RAINBOW magic

PET FAIRIES 1-4

KATIE
the Kitten Fairy

BELLA
the Bunny Fairy

GEORGIA
the Guinea Pig Fairy

LAUREN
the Puppy Fairy

By Daisy Meadows

Illustrated by Georgie Ripper

Silver Dolphin

Silver Dolphin

Silver Dolphin Books
An imprint of Printers Row Publishing Group
A division of Readerlink Distribution Services, LLC
9717 Pacific Heights Blvd, San Diego, CA 92121
www.silverdolphinbooks.com

Copyright © 2022 Rainbow Magic Limited

Printers Row Publishing Group is a division of Readerlink Distribution Services, LLC.
Silver Dolphin Books is a registered trademark of Readerlink Distribution Services, LLC.

All notations of errors or omissions should be addressed to Silver Dolphin Books, Editorial Department, at the above address. All other correspondence (author inquiries, permissions) concerning the content of this book should be addressed to:
Hachette Children's Group
Carmelite House
50 Victoria Embankment
London
EC4Y 0DZ

Library of Congress Control Number: 2022939595

ISBN: 978-1-6672-0257-0
Manufactured, printed, and assembled in Heshan, China.
First printing, September 2022. LP/09/22
26 25 24 23 22 1 2 3 4 5

Table of Contents

KATIE
the Kitten Fairy   7

BELLA
the Bunny Fairy   77

GEORGIA
the Guinea Pig Fairy   149

LAUREN
the Puppy Fairy   219

KATIE
THE KITTEN FAIRY

Fairies with their pets I see
and yet no pet has chosen me!
So I will get some of my own
to share my perfect frosty home.

This spell I cast, its aim is clear:
To bring the magic pets straight here.
The Pet Fairies soon will see
their seven pets living with me!

Table of Contents

A VERY UNUSUAL KITTEN   11

SURPRISE ATTACK!   25

MISSING PETS!   35

GIRLS ON GUARD   45

SHIMMER'S PLAN   55

GRASPING GOBLINS   67

A VERY UNUSUAL KITTEN

"Catch!"

Kirsty Tate tossed a baseball into the air. She watched as her friend Rachel Walker ran across the grass to catch it. It was the first day of spring break and Rachel had come to stay with Kirsty's family for a whole week. The two girls were in the

park while Kirsty's parents were at the grocery store. The sun was shining brightly, and there wasn't a cloud in the sky. It felt like perfect spring weather.

Rachel held up the ball triumphantly. "Your turn," she called. "Ready?"

Before Kirsty could reply, loud barking rang through the air. Both girls spun around to see a large black dog bounding past them.

Rachel jumped back as the dog raced by. "Is that a squirrel it's chasing?" she asked, watching the dog run off.

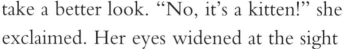

Kirsty shielded her eyes from the sun to take a better look. "No, it's a kitten!" she exclaimed. Her eyes widened at the sight of a tiny, gray kitten scrambling across the grass. "What's a kitten doing in the park?"

"I don't know—but that dog's about to catch it," Rachel said in alarm. "Come on!"

The two girls started to run after the animals. But they hadn't gotten very far before a sudden flash of bright light flickered through the air. A cloud of amber-colored sparkles swirled around the kitten. Seconds later, the kitten vanished—and an enormous striped tiger appeared in its place! The tiger turned toward the dog and roared.

Right away, the dog stopped short and put its ears back. Then, with a frightened whimper, it turned and bolted away as quickly as it could.

Kirsty and Rachel watched in disbelief as the tiger turned back into a kitten with another flash of bright sparkles.

The kitten shook itself off, licked one paw, and padded off happily through the grass.

Rachel rubbed
her eyes. "Did
you just see that?"
she asked, her
eyes still fixed on
the kitten.

Kirsty nodded.
"That looked like
fairy magic!" she
exclaimed.

Rachel grinned.
"That's exactly
what I thought,"
she replied. Whenever she and Kirsty
were together, they always had the best
magical adventures. This looked like it
might be the start of another one!

Then Rachel paused thoughtfully. "But
. . . we haven't seen any fairies here!"

Kirsty frowned. "That is strange, isn't it?" she said. "Let's follow the kitten. Maybe it will lead us to a fairy!"

The two girls hurried after the small kitten. It didn't seem to be in any real rush as it wandered along, stopping to pounce on a daisy or bat at a blade of grass.

"Where do you think its going?" Rachel whispered. "It seems like it's heading right for that fence."

They both watched as the kitten walked cheerfully toward a wooden fence at the edge of the grass. The fence was too high for the kitten to climb over, but it showed no sign of changing direction.

"How is the kitten going to—" Kirsty started. Then she broke off in surprise.

With another swirl of sparkles, the kitten had suddenly shrunk! Now it was the size of a mouse, small enough to squeeze through a tiny hole at the bottom of the fence.

Kirsty's eyes widened as she watched its little gray tail disappear through the hole.

"Wow!" Rachel gasped, staring after the kitten. "Quick—there's a gate in the fence over that way. We can't lose track of that kitten!"

Both girls rushed through the gate, and saw that the kitten was now full-size again. The only sign that it had ever been any different was a faint trail of magical sparkles glimmering behind it.

Just then, the kitten twitched its whiskers and bounded toward a food cart. As the girls got closer, they saw it run up to a man who was standing by the vendor.

"Fish sticks and fries, please," the girls heard him say.

The kitten meowed loudly. It wound itself between the man's legs as the vendor handed him a plateful of food.

The man chuckled. "Sorry, kitty," he said, sitting down on a nearby bench. "This is my lunch, not yours."

As the man began to eat, Kirsty elbowed Rachel and nodded toward the kitten. Its eyes were glowing a bright green.

A small cloud of amber-colored sparkles glittered in the air as the kitten looked up hopefully at the man's food.

A second later, a fish stick tumbled off the man's plate and landed at the kitten's feet!

With a happy meow, the kitten pounced on the fish stick and began to eat it.

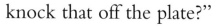

The man laughed. "It's your lucky day, kitty," he said. "How did I knock that off the plate?"

Rachel and Kirsty grinned at each other. They knew that the sneaky kitten had used magic to make the fish stick fall to the ground.

"That was definitely fairy magic!" Kirsty exclaimed. She watched as the kitten gobbled up the fish stick, cleaned its whiskers, and trotted off down a tree-lined path.

"Yes," Rachel agreed. "Something strange is going on! Let's see where the kitten goes now." The girls set off after the kitten again.

They hadn't gotten far when they heard a scuffling sound along the side of the path. Suddenly, six green goblins jumped out from behind a tree! They were clutching butterfly nets.

"There it is!" shouted one of the goblins, pointing at the kitten. "Get it!"

SURPRISE ATTACK!

"Goblins!" Kirsty cried in surprise.
"Oh, no!"

At the sight of the goblins, the
kitten's fur stood up like a prickly brush.
It hissed at the goblins, then turned and
ran away from them, toward the girls.
With nowhere else to go, it leaped right
up into Rachel's arms!

"Oh!" Rachel gasped, surprised to find the little bundle of fur in her arms. She held the kitten protectively as the goblins approached.

"Give us that kitten!" one of the them ordered. "It belongs to Jack Frost, and we've been sent to bring it home," he added.

Kirsty and Rachel hesitated. They'd met Jack Frost's goblins many times before, and knew what sneaky creatures they could be. Could they really trust the goblins to be telling the truth?

The kitten gave a soft meow, and both girls looked down at it. Its eyes were shining bright green again. Sparkles streamed out of its mouth and swirled around in the air! The kitten meowed again, but this time the girls could hear words in its meows.

"Don't believe those terrible goblins," the kitten declared. "I belong to Katie the Kitten Fairy, but I'm lost!"

Kirsty's fingers quickly closed over the locket around her neck. She and Rachel had been given matching gold lockets full of fairy dust by the Fairy King and Queen. The fairy dust would take them straight to Fairyland if they ever needed help. Now seemed like a very good time to use the lockets!

"We don't believe you," Rachel told the goblins. "And you're not getting this kitten!" Just then, Kirsty threw golden fairy dust all over herself, Rachel, and the kitten.

With angry cries, two of the goblins dropped their butterfly nets and dove toward the girls. They stretched their gnarled green hands out to grab the kitten.

Rachel yelped and tried to dodge out of the way, but luckily, the fairy dust was already working its magic. The girls were swept up into the sky. Below them, the goblins pounced on empty air and fell onto the grass.

Rachel and Kirsty laughed in relief as they felt the fairy dust whisking them through the air. After a moment, they couldn't see the park below, just a blur of bright, sparkling colors all around them. Rachel held the kitten close, in case it was frightened. It seemed used to fairy magic, though, and snuggled up happily in Rachel's arms. Its little ears blew back in the warm, sparkly breeze.

Moments later, the girls floated softly down to the ground. As the magical breeze died away, they both smiled to see that they were back in Fairyland.

"We're fairies!" Rachel exclaimed happily, fluttering her delicate wings.

"And there's the fairy palace, and the king and queen!" Kirsty cheered, waving as King Oberon and Queen Titania approached. Then she frowned.

"They don't look very happy, though."

Rachel watched as the king and queen came closer, followed by a crowd of anxious-looking fairies. Her excitement at being back in Fairyland disappeared as she saw how unhappy they all looked. Something was clearly troubling them. What was wrong?

MISSING PETS!

"Hello, Your Majesties," Rachel said politely, giving the king and queen a curtsy with the kitten still in her arms. "Is everything all right?"

A fairy in a pale yellow dress with long, dark hair suddenly caught sight of the kitten. A happy smile lit up her face.

"You've brought Shimmer back!" she cried. "Oh, thank you, thank you!"

The kitten jumped out of Rachel's arms and scampered over to the pretty fairy. The fairy scooped her up, burying her face in Shimmer's soft, silky fur.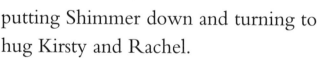

"Thank you so much," she said, putting Shimmer down and turning to hug Kirsty and Rachel.

"I'm Katie the Kitten Fairy, and I can't tell you how glad I am to see Shimmer back in Fairyland!"

"You're welcome," Rachel said, smiling.

The king and queen stepped forward.

"How nice to see you again, girls," the king said warmly. "These are our Pet Fairies. You've already met Katie. This is Bella the Bunny Fairy, Georgia the Guinea Pig Fairy, Lauren the Puppy Fairy, Harriet the Hamster Fairy, Molly the Goldfish Fairy, and Penny the Pony Fairy."

Each fairy stepped forward when her name was called and curtsied to the girls with a little smile. Kirsty couldn't help noticing that their smiles looked a bit sad.

"So where are all the other pets?" she asked curiously.

The fairies all sighed. "Jack Frost stole them," Queen Titania told the girls sadly. "He took them to his ice castle, then sent out a ransom note. It said that if the Pet Fairies couldn't find him a pet of his own, he would keep all their magic pets for himself."

"Oh, no!" Kirsty cried out. "He can't do that!"

"He already has," the king responded. "And without their magic pets, the Pet Fairies can't look after all the pets in your world."

"The Pet Fairies are responsible for helping pets that are lost or homeless," the queen explained. "But they can't do that if their own magic pets are missing."

"Can't we give Jack Frost another pet, so that he'll let the magic pets go?" Rachel suggested.

The queen shook her head. "I'm afraid it's not that simple." She sighed. "In Fairyland, pets *choose* their owners. And no pet has ever chosen Jack Frost."

"I'm not surprised!" Kirsty blurted out. Jack Frost was always causing trouble in Fairyland. No wonder none of the magic pets wanted to live with him!

The king was gazing at Shimmer with a thoughtful expression on his face. "Kirsty, Rachel, where did you find Shimmer?" he asked. "We thought all the magic pets were locked in Jack Frost's ice castle."

"She was wandering around in the local park," Kirsty replied. "She looked lost!"

The kitten gave a sudden loud meow, as if she was joining in the conversation. Katie listened hard, then nodded. "Shimmer says that all the magic pets were all being kept in Jack Frost's castle," she said. "But they managed to escape, and now they're all roaming around in the human world."

The Pet Fairies looked very happy to hear this, but Shimmer was still meowing.

Katie listened again, then bit her lip. "Jack Frost has sent out a group of goblins to catch them and take them back to the ice castle," she announced anxiously. "Oh, our poor little pets!"

The other Pet Fairies gasped, and the king and queen looked worried, too.

"We have to find the pets before the goblins do!" the queen said, sounding determined.

Kirsty and Rachel looked at each other. Then, at the same time, they said, "We'll help!"

GIRLS ON GUARD

All the fairies cheered when the girls agreed to help.

"Thank you!" King Oberon said, smiling. "It's very kind of you to help us once again."

"The magic pets may be hard to find," Queen Titania warned them. "In Fairyland, they are tiny, fairy-size pets, but in the human world, they can be any size they wish. They can also work some fairy magic of their own, so you will have to look very carefully."

Shimmer meowed suddenly and Katie bent her head to listen. Her face turned serious. "Shimmer said that a kitten in the human world needs our help," she told the others. "It has no home. Shimmer and I need to find one for it!" Katie turned to the king and queen. "Can we go rescue the kitten?"

The king and queen both hesitated. "We'd love you to help . . ." the queen began slowly.

"But we don't want the goblins to catch Shimmer," the king finished.

"Maybe we could go with Katie and Shimmer," Kirsty suggested. "We could protect them from the goblins!"

The king and queen looked at each other.

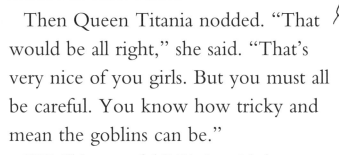

Then Queen Titania nodded. "That would be all right," she said. "That's very nice of you girls. But you must all be careful. You know how tricky and mean the goblins can be."

"We'll be careful," Katie said, her face lighting up. "Let's go!" She waved her wand, and a trail of amber-colored fairy dust trailed from it.

The dust trickled down around Kirsty and Rachel, and suddenly, Fairyland blurred before their eyes. A magical wind swept them up, and they flew through the air with Katie and Shimmer.

In a rush of color and light, the girls found themselves back in their own world. They were human-size once again!

"We're back in the park," Rachel said, looking around. "Watch out for goblins, everyone!"

Katie was still holding tiny Shimmer. She flew to hide on Kirsty's shoulder while the girls looked around for goblins.

The magic kitten jumped down from Katie's arms and curled up on Kirsty's shoulder. Kirsty could feel his little tail twitching back and forth.

"That tickles!" Kirsty giggled as Shimmer batted playfully at her hair.

"The coast is clear," Rachel said, after the girls scanned the park. "Let's start looking for a homeless kitten."

"We'll have to search carefully," Katie advised. "If it's scared, it could have hidden somewhere."

The four of them set off, keeping their ears open for meows. Katie flew between the girls at shoulder height, while Shimmer padded along beside her in midair.

How fascinating to watch him, Kirsty thought.

Even though the tiny kitten was hovering magically in the air, he moved as if he were on the ground. Sometimes he padded along, occasionally he pounced, and every so often he stopped to stalk a floating dandelion seed, or to chase his own fluffy tail. He seemed particularly interested in the elastic holding Rachel's ponytail, which had a couple of pink stars dangling from it. A few times, he leaped up to catch the stars between his tiny paws.

"Come on, Shimmer, we've got work to do," Katie reminded him.

She fluttered over to scoop him out of Rachel's hair. "Where could that lost kitten be?"

Suddenly, Shimmer pricked up his ears and stopped. His little pink nose turned up and his whiskers twitched as he sniffed the air. Then he took a flying leap down to the ground in a bright burst of sparkles, and he grew to the size of a normal kitten! Shimmer raced off ahead of the girls toward the playground.

"I think he found the kitten!" Katie smiled, flying behind her pet. "Come on, girls!"

Rachel and Kirsty ran after Shimmer as he bolted through the grass. Just before he reached the playground, he swerved toward a tall elm tree and sat at the bottom, looking up at it.

Kirsty, Rachel, and Katie gazed up to see what Shimmer had found. On one of the highest branches, huddled against the trunk and looking down at them with big golden eyes, sat a tiny tabby kitten.

SHIMMER'S PLAN

"Poor little thing!" Kirsty exclaimed. "It's only a baby!"

Just then, a breeze blew through the tree, and the tabby kitten pounced on a leaf that was flapping nearby. It almost lost its balance and tumbled out of the tree!

"Careful, kitty," Katie called up. The kitten sat down and started washing its paws.

Shimmer ran a little way up the tree toward the tabby kitten and started meowing. The kitten meowed back eagerly.

"Oh, the poor kitten climbed the tree to get out of the wind last night and now it's stuck!" Katie translated Shimmer and the other kitten's meows.

"It's too scared to climb back down." "Should I climb up and get it?" Rachel offered. Before Katie could reply, Shimmer started meowing again. The fairy listened, then looked over at the nearby playground. "Good idea, Shimmer," she said, smiling. Then she turned back to the girls. "Thanks for the offer, Rachel, but Shimmer has someone else in mind for the job," she explained with a grin.

She pointed her wand in the direction of the playground. "See that boy in a red shirt at the top of the jungle gym?" she asked.

"The one with black hair?" Kirsty said, squinting.

Katie nodded. "That's the one," she  replied. "Would you go and ask him if he can help you get the kitten down from the tree?"

"OK," Kirsty agreed, confused.

"Trust me," Katie said. "It's very important that it is that boy who rescues this kitten." She winked at the girls. Shimmer meowed loudly, as if he was agreeing with Katie.

"All right," Rachel laughed. "Come on, Kirsty!"

Shimmer shrank back down to fairy pet size. He and Katie hid in the tree while Rachel and Kirsty ran over to the playground. The dark-haired boy had just jumped off the jungle gym when the girls arrived.

"Hello," Kirsty said, giving him a friendly smile. "I'm Kirsty, and this is Rachel. Could you help us rescue a kitten? It's stuck in a tree."

"We saw how good you are at climbing," Rachel explained. "We were wondering if you could climb up the tree and get it down?"

"Sure," the boy replied eagerly. "My name is James, and I love cats. Where's the kitten?"

The girls pointed out the elm tree. James yelled over to tell his dad to let him know where he was going. Then he followed Kirsty and Rachel to the tree.

James looked up at the
kitten. "Don't worry,
little kitten! I'll have
you down in two
minutes," he
called and
began to climb.

Kirsty and
Rachel watched
as he clambered
higher and
higher. Just as
he was about to
reach the branch
that the tabby
kitten was perched
on, the kitten jumped
down onto James's shoulder and butted
its head gently against the boy's cheek.

Kirsty blinked. It looked like a haze of amber-colored sparkles surrounded James and the kitten. She glanced at Rachel and they grinned knowingly—more Pet Fairy magic!

James carefully carried the tabby kitten all the way back down to the ground. "It's so tiny," he marveled, stroking the kitten gently. "I wonder where it lives."

"It doesn't have a collar or a nametag," Kirsty said. "It looks like a stray."

"Here comes my dad," James said, as a tall, dark-haired man strolled

over. "Dad, look! We found a lost kitten!" His eyes brightened suddenly. "Hey, Dad—can we keep it?"

James's dad smiled. "Your mom and I have been talking about getting you a pet," he said. "But we can't just take this one without checking to make sure it doesn't belong to someone else." He looked around to see if the kitten's owner was somewhere in the park.

"We've been here for awhile," Kirsty said politely. "Nobody seems to be looking for the kitten."

"Please?" James asked quickly, as soon as his dad hesitated. "We can take it home with us, and call the animal shelter from our house." He stroked it again. "Oh, it's purring, Dad. It likes me!"

James's dad ruffled his son's hair. "OK then," he said. "If nobody's reported the kitten missing, then I think you can keep it."

"Hooray!" cheered James, beaming from ear to ear. He tickled the tabby kitten under its chin, and the kitten purred even louder. "Do you think Dusty would be a good name?" James wondered aloud.

Rachel nudged Kirsty. She had spotted a few more flecks of fairy dust twinkling in the air around James and the kitten! "Oh, Dusty would be a wonderful name," she said, trying not to giggle.

"Well, then, Dusty," James's dad said, petting the kitten, "we'd better take you home!"

GRASPING GOBLINS

The girls watched as James and his dad walked away happily with their new kitten.

"Good work, girls!" Katie exclaimed as she came out from her hiding place in the tree. "I think Dusty and James will be very happy together."

Shimmer scampered along a tree branch, purring loudly to show that he agreed, and the girls laughed.

"Fairy magic is wonderful!" Rachel said with a smile. She watched as Shimmer sniffed at a beetle on a nearby leaf and gave a tiny, fairy-sized sneeze.

Just then, Kirsty heard a rustling sound from a little higher up in the tree. She looked up to see a goblin— and then another— and then another! She gasped. There was a whole chain of grinning goblins hanging down from one branch of the tree! The lowest goblin was dangling just above the branch where Shimmer was perched. He was reaching out to grab the magic kitten!

"No, you don't!" cried Kirsty,
scooping up Shimmer, just in time.

"Give it here!" the goblin growled,
lunging after the kitten.

Shimmer meowed in alarm as the goblin's fingers came within a whisker of him. But the goblin had reached out too far, and the other goblins couldn't hold on to him. They all tumbled to the ground, landing in a big green pile of tangled arms and legs!

"Ouch! You're squishing me!" grumbled one goblin.

"Get off!" groaned another.

Katie grinned at the girls. "Come on! Let's go while we have the chance," she said.

Kirsty held out her hands and let Shimmer run through the air to Katie as they all walked away from the pile of grumpy goblins. "I don't think Jack Frost will be pleased when they come back empty-handed," Kirsty said, glancing back over her shoulder.

The goblins were still bickering!

"No, Jack Frost won't be happy," Katie agreed. She suddenly shivered. "He'll send them out again to look for another pet." She cuddled her kitten tightly at the thought of it. "Let's get you safely back to Fairyland, Shimmer," she said in her sweet voice. "Good-bye girls—and thank you for everything."

Katie hugged the girls in turn, and then Shimmer nuzzled his tiny nose against each of their faces.

"Good-bye, little Shimmer," Kirsty said, giggling as his fur tickled her nose.

"It's been nice to meet you."

"Tell the other Pet Fairies that we'll keep looking for the other lost pets," Rachel added, blowing Katie and Shimmer a kiss.

"We will," Katie promised. "Good-bye!" She tucked Shimmer carefully under one arm, then waved her wand. A shower of amber-colored lights twinkled around Katie and Shimmer, and then they were gone.

Rachel and Kirsty smiled at each other and headed home. After all the excitement, they both felt hungry. "I'm so happy we found a nice home for Dusty," Rachel said with a smile. "Everything worked out perfectly. It couldn't have gone better!"

Kirsty slipped her arm through Rachel's as they walked out the park gate.

"I can't wait to find another one of the lost fairy pets," she said excitedly. "It looks like another fairy adventure isn't far away!"

BELLA
THE BUNNY FAIRY

FAIRIES WITH THEIR PETS I SEE
AND YET NO PET HAS CHOSEN ME!
SO I WILL GET SOME OF MY OWN
TO SHARE MY PERFECT FROSTY HOME.

THIS SPELL I CAST, ITS AIM IS CLEAR:
TO BRING THE MAGIC PETS STRAIGHT HERE.
THE PET FAIRIES SOON WILL SEE
THEIR SEVEN PETS LIVING WITH ME!

Katie's kitten Shimmer has been found.
Now Kirsty and Rachel need to help find
BELLA'S BUNNY, MISTY.

Table of Contents

EASTER BUNNY   81

VANISHING ACT   93

BELLA FLIES IN   105

BUNNIES EVERYWHERE!   113

GOBLINS CHASE!   123

A MAGICAL EASTER   135

EASTER
BUNNY

"Isn't it a perfect day for a party?" Kirsty
Tate said, looking up at the sapphire-blue
sky.

Her best friend, Rachel Walker,
nodded and handed Kirsty a chocolate
egg. Rachel was staying with Kirsty
for spring break, and the girls were busy
hiding eggs. They were getting ready for

Jane, Mr. and Mrs. Dillon's five-year-old daughter. The Dillons lived down the street from Kirsty.

"There are some great hiding places here," Rachel said. She gazed around the beautiful yard full of green grass and colorful flower beds. Then she knelt down and hid the egg under a shrub. "Jane and her friends will love the Easter egg hunt!"

"It'll be fun," Kirsty agreed, hiding an egg behind the birdbath.

"How many children are invited to the party?" Rachel asked.

"Eleven!" Kirsty replied, her eyes twinkling. "Mr. and Mrs. Dillon are so glad that we're helping! They've been friends with my mom and dad for a long time, and Jane is really sweet." Then she lowered her voice. "Do you think we'll find another of the missing fairy pets today, Rachel?"

"I hope so," Rachel whispered back.

"Let's keep our eyes open!"

Rachel and Kirsty had a special secret. They were best friends with the fairies! Whenever there was trouble in Fairyland, the girls were always happy to help. But trouble usually meant that mean Jack Frost and his goblins were up to no good.

This time, Jack Frost had been angry because he didn't have a pet of his own. He had kidnapped the seven magical animals belonging to the Pet Fairies! The pets had all been taken to his ice castle, but the mischievous pets had escaped into the human world. Jack Frost then sent his goblins to capture the pets and bring them back!

Without their magic animals, the Pet Fairies couldn't help pets in the human world that were lost or in danger.

The girls were determined to find the fairy pets before Jack Frost's goblins did!

"Well, we've gotten off to a good start," Kirsty pointed out. "Katie the Kitten Fairy was so happy when we returned her magic kitten, Shimmer."

Just then, a pretty little girl with long blonde curls waved to the friends from the back door. "Hi, Kirsty! Hi, Rachel!" she called. She had been upstairs changing into her pink party dress when the girls arrived. Now she rushed toward them, her face bright with excitement.

"All my friends are coming to the party, Kirsty! We're going to have an Easter egg hunt, and then Mommy and Daddy are giving me a special Easter present!" she said excitedly.

"You're so lucky, Jane!" Kirsty smiled as Mr. and Mrs. Dillon followed their daughter into the yard.

"Jane, let's go get the presents ready for your guests," said Mrs. Dillon, noticing that Rachel and Kirsty still had some chocolate eggs to hide. "I think Rachel and Kirsty are busy!"

She and Jane went back inside, and Mr. Dillon turned to the girls. "It's really nice of you to help out," he said gratefully. "There's so much to do." Then he smiled. "Would you like to see Jane's Easter present?"

The girls nodded, and Mr. Dillon led them to the garage. Inside, sitting on the workbench, was a cardboard box with little holes in it.

Rachel and Kirsty peeked inside and saw
a fluffy black rabbit with floppy ears,
nestled on
a bed of straw.

"Oh, it's so
cute!" Rachel
gasped.

"Jane will love
it," Kirsty added.

Mr. Dillon
smiled. "Yes, she will," he agreed.
"She's been pestering us for a rabbit!"

Rachel turned to Kirsty. "We'd
better finish hiding the eggs," she said.
"The guests will be here soon! Thanks for
showing us the surprise, Mr. Dillon."

Quickly, the girls hid the remaining eggs
behind flowerpots, trees, and the shed.
Just as Kirsty placed the last egg behind

a clump of daffodils, she heard the front
doorbell ring.

"Here they come!" Rachel said with
a grin.

Fifteen minutes later, all the guests had
arrived. Jane was dashing around the
garden with her friends, looking for the
chocolate eggs.

"I've found one!" Jane shouted, her
cheeks glowing.

"Good job!" Kirsty laughed. She and Rachel were watching from the patio. There were shrieks of delight as some of the other children found eggs too.

"Oh!" A little girl in a yellow dress suddenly gasped loudly. "Come look!"

Rachel and Kirsty hurried over to the girl. She was kneeling down in front of a tree, peering at the trunk.

"I just saw the Easter Bunny!" she announced breathlessly.

Rachel and Kirsty stared at her, confused. They hadn't hidden a toy rabbit anywhere!

"Where?" asked Rachel.

The little girl pointed at a hole in the tree trunk. "It came out of there, but then it popped back in again," she said.

"How do you know it was the Easter Bunny?" Kirsty asked.

"Because it was bright pink!" the little girl replied.

Rachel and Kirsty glanced at each other in surprise. Then Rachel looked more closely at the hole in the tree. Suddenly, her heart began to race. She was sure she could see the faintest glimmer of fairy magic!

VANISHING ACT

Rachel nudged Kirsty, who had just sent the little girl off to look for more eggs. "Look!" she whispered.

Kirsty stared at the shimmering, magical haze in front of the tree trunk, and her eyes lit up. "Fairy magic!" she gasped. "Rachel, do you think—"

But before Kirsty could finish, there was another shout from across the yard.

"I saw the Easter bunny too!"
A little boy was pointing at a large, leafy shrub and beaming with pride.

Kirsty and Rachel ran over to him. They could hardly believe their eyes.

There was a beautiful, fluffy, lilac-colored rabbit, sitting under the shrub! But as Kirsty bent to move the leaves out of the way, the rabbit vanished in a glittering cloud of purple sparkles.

"This is definitely fairy magic!" Kirsty whispered. "The bunny must be one of the fairy pets!"

"Yes, I bet it's Bella the Bunny Fairy's rabbit!" Rachel agreed.

By now, all the children wanted to see the Easter Bunny.

"Where did the bunny go?" asked one little girl, looking disappointed.

"I don't know," Kirsty replied quickly. "Why don't you go and look for more eggs until we find out?"

"Let's look for the Easter bunny instead!" Jane suggested. All the children cheered.

They began racing around the yard, calling, "Bunny! Where are you?"

"We have to find the rabbit and get it back to Bella," Kirsty whispered to Rachel. "Luckily, I don't see any goblins around! I wonder where the bunny is now?"

Suddenly, Rachel's eyes widened. She grabbed her friend's arm. "Look at the picnic table!"

Mr. and Mrs. Dillon had put the party food out on the table while the children searched for eggs. They had just gone

back inside to get more. But as the girls stared, they could see a swirl of golden sparkles hovering over the food!

The girls hurried to the table. Sitting next to a big plate of salad, nibbling on a carrot, was the magic bunny. And now, it was a sunshine-yellow color!

Before Kirsty and Rachel could do anything, Jane spotted the rabbit too.

"The Easter bunny!" she shouted. The whole group of children rushed over to the table.

"Be careful," Rachel said anxiously. Would the bunny disappear again if it got scared?

But Jane stepped up to the table and gently stroked the rabbit's fluffy head. It seemed quite happy to have someone pet it. "Isn't it cute?" Jane said with a sigh. "I wish I had my very own bunny!"

"We'd better get the rabbit away before Mr. and Mrs. Dillon come back out," Kirsty whispered to Rachel. "I don't know how we'll explain a yellow bunny! We can take it to my house."

Rachel nodded. "The bunny's very tired," she announced to Jane and her friends, picking it up gently. "It's going home now, so say good-bye."

"Good-bye, Easter bunny!" the children cried, waving. Then they dashed off to search for more Easter eggs.

"I'll tell the Dillons we have to run home for something," Kirsty murmured to Rachel, heading inside.

When she came
back outside, the
two girls carried
the bunny around
the house. They
went out through
the side gate and
closed it carefully
behind them.

"How are we
going to keep the
rabbit safe until
Bella the Bunny
Fairy gets here?"
asked Rachel as
the girls walked along
an overgrown path next to the house.

"She can't be far away," Kirsty replied.
"But maybe we could use the fairy dust in

our magic lockets to take the bunny back to Fairyland ourselves."

Before Rachel could reply, the girls heard a nasty chuckling sound above their heads. Alarmed, they looked up. Four green goblins were sitting on the branch of a large oak tree, grinning down at them!

"Oh, no!" Rachel gasped.

"Let's get out of here!" Kirsty whispered.

The two girls hurried along the path. But all of a sudden, the ground beneath their feet seemed to disappear.

"Help!" Kirsty cried as she tumbled into a large hole.

Rachel was too shocked to yell, but luckily she managed to keep hold of the magic rabbit as she fell. The two girls landed on a bed of soft leaves and looked at each other in horror.

"The goblins must have dug this hole
and covered it with branches!" Kirsty
gasped. "They set a trap!"

"And we walked right into it!"
Rachel groaned.

"Ha ha ha!" The goblins cackled
gleefully, peering down at the girls.

"We were trying to catch the magic
bunny, but we also caught two pesky girls
as well!" one goblin cried. "Hooray!"

BELLA FLIES IN

As Rachel and Kirsty climbed to their feet, the goblins bent over the hole. Before the girls could stop them, one of the goblins reached down and snatched the magic rabbit out of Rachel's hands. The bunny squirmed in dismay.

"Give that bunny back!" Rachel shouted, trying to climb up out of the hole.

The goblins ran around the side
of the house toward the
front yard, laughing
and cheering as they went.

"We can't let them
get away!" Kirsty said
urgently, trying to
pull herself out of
the hole too. But
it was just a *little*
too deep for the
girls to climb
out of.

Just then,
a silvery voice
echoed through the
air. "Hang on girls, I'm
coming!"

Rachel and Kirsty looked up.

A tiny fairy surfed through the air toward them on a large green oak leaf. Her long hair streamed out behind her in the breeze. "It's Bella the Bunny Fairy!" Kirsty said happily. Bella came to a stop above Rachel's and Kirsty's heads and waved at them. She wore a beautiful, green dress, beaded sunflowers at her waist and neck, and gold shoes.

"We're so glad to see you, Bella," Rachel said gratefully. "But I'm afraid the goblins have run off with your bunny. We're so sorry!"

Bella nodded. "I knew Misty was around here somewhere!" she exclaimed. "Don't worry, those goblins can't have gone far. I'll have you girls out of there in two twitches of a bunny's nose!"

She lifted her wand, and a shower of golden sparkles floated down onto the girls. Rachel and Kirsty held their breath as they shrank to fairy size, and glittering wings appeared on their backs.

"Great idea, Bella!" Rachel laughed as she flew easily out of the hole, with Kirsty beside her.

"What should we do now?" asked Kirsty. The three friends hovered in midair, wings fluttering.

"How will we find the goblins?"

Just then a gruff, angry shout rang out across the yard.

"Follow that sound!" Bella cried, swooping through the air toward the front of the house.

Rachel and Kirsty hurried behind her. Within moments, the three of them peered around the corner of the house, into the front yard.

The goblins were crouched behind some bushes under an open window. They were arguing fiercely. One of them, the biggest goblin, was holding Misty.

"There's my bunny!" Bella whispered, pointing at the frightened-looking rabbit. "Girls, we have to save her!"

BUNNIES EVERYWHERE!

The goblins hadn't noticed Rachel, Kirsty, and Bella watching them. They were too busy arguing.

"You do it!" one snarled.

"No, you do it!" another replied.

"I'm not climbing up there!" The first goblin said, pointing at the open window. "I might fall and hurt myself!"

"Coward!" jeered the goblin holding Misty.

"What are they arguing about?" Rachel whispered.

"Look!" Kirsty replied, pointing at the open kitchen window. A big basket of chocolate Easter eggs sat on the windowsill. "You know how greedy goblins are. They want those chocolate eggs!"

Under the window was
a wooden trellis with
roses growing on it.
One of the goblins
tried to climb the
trellis, but it swayed
slightly. He jumped
off, nervous.

"What's the matter
with you?" another
goblin sneered.
"Scaredy cat!"

"Am not!" the
climbing goblin roared furiously.

"Poor Misty!" Bella said, staring
anxiously at her bunny. "She's shaking
with fear."

"Why can't she just disappear like she
did before?" asked Kirsty.

Bella shook her head sadly. "Misty can't disappear if someone's holding her, or if she's scared," she explained. "We have to figure out a way to get her back!"

While Kirsty and Bella were talking, Rachel had been looking at the basket of chocolate eggs. In the middle of it sat a beautiful, blue toy bunny. It looked a lot like Misty! Just then, Rachel had an idea.

Excited, she turned to the little fairy. "Bella, I think there might be a way to get back Misty!

Can you make Kirsty and me human-size again?"

Bella nodded. She waved her wand, and in an instant the two girls were back to normal.

"We need to go inside the house," Rachel whispered.

Confused, Kirsty and Bella followed Rachel back to the side gate. As Rachel opened it, Bella fluttered down and hid in her pocket.

Then the girls walked into the backyard, where the children were still looking for eggs. Mr. and Mrs. Dillon were putting

plates out on the picnic table.

"Mrs. Dillon, is it OK if I borrow the blue bunny from the Easter egg basket in the kitchen? I promise to return it," Rachel asked.

Mrs. Dillon looked surprised, but she said it was all right.

Rachel and Kirsty smiled at her and went inside to the kitchen. Rachel peeked out the window and saw the goblins still arguing down below. Then she picked up the blue toy bunny and gave the basket a little tap. Several of the chocolate eggs fell

out and tumbled to the ground outside
the window.

"That'll keep the goblins busy for a few
more minutes!" Rachel said quietly.

Kirsty looked over the windowsill. The
goblins had pounced on the chocolate
eggs and were gobbling them up.

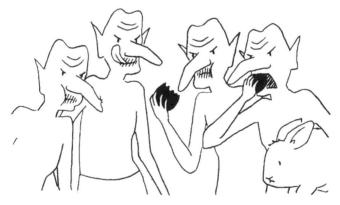

"Time to head back outside now,"
Rachel whispered. Kirsty followed her
friend out of the house, through the side
gate, and over to the hole in the path that
the goblins had made.

"Kirsty, can you cover the hole with twigs and leaves like the goblins did?" Rachel asked.

Kirsty nodded and began pulling some fallen branches over the hole.

"Bella, we need a long piece of string," said Rachel. "Can you help?"

"Of course!" Bella agreed, zooming out of Rachel's pocket. She waved her wand. In a shower of sparkles, a long piece of golden string appeared on the path.

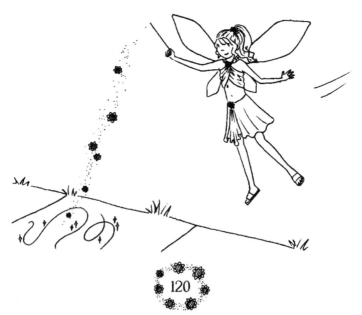

Rachel grabbed the string. She tied
one end of it around the middle of the
toy bunny. Kirsty and Bella watched
in amazement. They didn't have a clue
what Rachel was up to!

"We're all set!" Rachel grinned as she
finished tying the knot. "Now all we
need is Misty's help to make sure my
plan works!"

GOBLINS CHASE!

"Tell me what Misty has to do," Bella said eagerly.

"We need her to escape from the goblins for a few minutes," Rachel explained, waving the toy bunny in the air. "Then we'll try to confuse them with this!"

"You mean, we'll make the goblins

think the toy is Misty?" Kirsty said. "But to do that, Misty will need to be—"

"Blue!" Bella laughed. "No problem!" Lifting her wand, she began to write in the air with it. Like a sparkler, the wand left a glittering trail of bright blue letters, the exact same color as the toy bunny. The letters spelled out:

"Perfect!" Rachel declared, grinning.

"Now Misty knows exactly what color blue she has to be!" Bella said with a smile. As the words hovered in midair, she flicked her wand and sent them floating around the side of the house, toward her pet. The girls followed, eager to see what would happen. They could hear the goblins squabbling loudly.

"That's mine! Give it back!"

"You've had lots, greedy Gus!"

"Who are you calling greedy Gus?"

The goblins were still fighting over the chocolate eggs.

125

Rachel and Kirsty peeked around the side of the house as Bella's message floated toward Misty. They saw the little bunny's nose twitch. And then, very slowly, the sunshine-yellow of her fluffy coat began to turn exactly the same shade of blue as the toy bunny! At the same time, Bella's magic message faded in the air.

Suddenly, one of the goblins noticed that Misty was bright blue. He could hardly believe his eyes. "Look!" he yelled, jumping up and down. "The bunny turned blue!" He stared suspiciously at the big goblin holding Misty.

"What did you do to it?"

"Nothing!" the big goblin snapped. "It's not my fault!"

"Ha ha!" one of the others laughed smugly. "If Jack Frost wanted a yellow bunny instead of a blue one, you're going to be in big trouble!"

As the goblins began arguing about who'd changed the rabbit's color, Rachel put the toy bunny on the ground. She held onto the other end of the string and turned to Bella.

"Please turn Kirsty and me into fairies again!" she whispered.

As soon as Rachel and Kirsty had their wings back, the girls fluttered up into the air. Kirsty helped Rachel hold the end of the string. The toy bunny was too heavy for Rachel to carry now that she was fairy-size!

"We need Misty to escape and lead the goblins over here," Rachel told Bella.

Bella nodded and began to write in the air with her wand again. This time, the message said:

FOLLOW ME

Rachel, Kirsty, and Bella watched as
the message floated around the side of
the house toward Misty. The goblins
were pushing and shoving one another
now. The one with Misty in his arms
was so annoyed that he was jumping up
and down in anger. The girls could see
that he wasn't holding the bunny very
tightly anymore.

As soon as Misty
saw Bella's message,
she began to wriggle
and kick. The
goblin was taken by
surprise! In a second,
Misty had squirmed
from his grasp and
was racing toward
the side of the house.

"You klutz!" the other goblins shouted angrily. "You've let the bunny go! After it!"

As Misty dashed around the side of the house toward Bella, she began to shrink to fairy-pet-size. Then the tiny blue rabbit scampered up off the ground! She lolloped happily through the air to Bella.

"Good job, Misty!" Bella cried. Rachel
and Kirsty smiled as the fairy gave her pet
a big hug. "Now come with me!"

As Bella and Misty flew off to hide
behind a tree, Rachel turned to Kirsty.
"Here come the goblins!" she whispered.
"Ready?"

Kirsty nodded.

A few seconds later, the goblins hurtled around the side of the house, grumbling and shouting.

"There she is!" shouted the big goblin, pointing at the toy bunny sitting on the path. "Get her!"

"Head toward the hole, Kirsty!" Rachel whispered.

The two girls began to fly, bouncing the blue bunny on its string along the ground below them. Rachel had been worried that the goblins might be able to see the string, but they couldn't. Their eyes were fixed on the toy rabbit. They charged after it—right toward the hole!

A MAGICAL EASTER

Rachel and Kirsty kept flying along, slowing down a little so that the goblins could get closer to the bunny. The girls bounced it carefully onto the twigs and leaves covering the hole.

"I'm going to catch it!" one of the goblins yelled triumphantly, reaching out for the bunny.

"No, let me!" shouted another.

"I want to tell Jack Frost that *I* caught it!" yelled a third.

All four goblins moved to grab the bunny at the same time. They fell on top of the twigs and leaves in a heap. A second later, the covering gave way. Yelping, the goblins all tumbled into the

hole. As they did, they pulled the string out of Rachel's and Kirsty's hands and took the toy bunny with them.

The girls grinned at each other proudly.

"What a great plan, Rachel!" Kirsty cried.

They flew down and hovered over the hole as the goblins climbed to their feet.

"Caught in our own trap!" the big goblin groaned.

"It's your fault!" one of the others snapped. "If you hadn't lost the bunny, we wouldn't be here now!"

"At least we've got the bunny back!" another added, picking the bunny up. Then he gave a screech of anger. "This isn't the magic bunny—it's a *toy*!"

Rachel and Kirsty laughed as he threw the toy rabbit out of the hole in disgust.

"It's a good thing goblins aren't too smart!" Rachel said. She and Kirsty flew over to join Misty and Bella, who had popped out from behind the nearby tree.

"Thank you, girls!" Bella laughed, her eyes sparkling with joy. "Misty is safe, and it's all thanks to you!"

"We were glad to help," Rachel replied.

Misty scampered down to Rachel's shoulder and nuzzled her ear gratefully. Then the bunny touched her nose to Kirsty's in thanks.

Suddenly, the tiny rabbit turned to Bella and began to twitch her nose furiously as she "talked" to her fairy owner.

"Girls," Bella announced after a moment, "Misty told me she came here because there's a bunny nearby that needs her help. It's lost!"

As Bella was speaking, Kirsty spotted something out of the corner of her eye: a small black bunny was poking its nose out of a nearby bush and staring up at her.

"Rachel, look!" She gasped. "I'm sure that's Jane's bunny. He must have escaped from its box!"

Rachel saw the black rabbit and nodded. "But how did it get out?" she wondered out loud.

"Kids, it's time for presents!" Mrs. Dillon's voice drifted over from the backyard, followed by cheers from the children.

Kirsty looked worried. "We have to get the bunny back into its box before Jane opens it!" she gasped.

"Bella, can you turn us back into girls again?" Rachel asked urgently.

Bella waved her wand right away. As soon as she was back to her normal size, Kirsty tiptoed across the grass toward the black bunny. It stared up at her with big dark eyes. To Kirsty's relief, the bunny let her pick it up.

"Let's go!" Rachel said, grabbing the toy bunny off the ground and untying the string.

Kirsty and Rachel hurried to the garage, while Bella and Misty flew in the air behind them.

The girls could see the children crowding around Mr. and Mrs. Dillon in the backyard, but luckily, nobody noticed them.

"Look!" Bella pointed her wand at the bunny's cardboard box. "That's how the bunny escaped!"

Rachel and Kirsty looked closer at the box and saw that a large hole had been chewed in one side. Carefully, Kirsty popped the little rabbit in through the hole. Then Bella waved her wand. A cloud of dazzling sparkles swirled around the box, making it whole again.

"Time for Jane's special present!"
Mr. Dillon announced, heading for the
garage.

"Let's get out of here!" Bella
whispered.

Quickly, they all hurried out of the
garage. They went back to the side gate
so that they could peek into the yard and
watch Jane open her present.

The little girl
looked very excited
when she saw the
box her dad put
down on the grass.
She pulled the flaps
open, and gave a
squeal of delight.

"A bunny! My
very own bunny!"

She reached in, gently
picked the rabbit up and
gave him a big hug.

"Look!" Kirsty
nudged Rachel. "Is
that just the sunshine,
or can you see a magical
sparkle around Jane and
her bunny?"

"Definitely a magical sparkle!" Rachel
said, grinning.

"I'm going to call him Sooty," Jane
laughed, beaming at her parents.

"Look at Misty!" Kirsty whispered
to Rachel.

The magical bunny looked just as happy
as Jane. Misty was so thrilled, she was
changing to all the colors of the rainbow,
from red to violet.

"It's time for us to go," Bella said, stroking Misty's fur. "Thanks so much for all your help, girls. Enjoy the rest of the party!"

She blew kisses at them, and Misty twitched her nose— one twitch for Rachel, and one for Kirsty. Then Bella waved her wand. She and Misty disappeared in a shower of fairy dust.

"Time for the chocolate eggs, kids!" Mrs. Dillon called.

Quickly, Rachel hurried over and popped the toy bunny back into the basket of eggs. The children crowded around Mrs. Dillon as she handed out the chocolate.

"The perfect end to a happy Easter!" Kirsty said.

Rachel smiled as she watched the children. "Yes," she agreed, grinning at Kirsty. "All the bunnies are with their proper owners!"

GEORGIA
THE GUINEA PIG FAIRY

149

FAIRIES WITH THEIR PETS I SEE
AND YET NO PET HAS CHOSEN ME!
SO I WILL GET SOME OF MY OWN
TO SHARE MY PERFECT FROSTY HOME.

THIS SPELL I CAST, ITS AIM IS CLEAR:
TO BRING THE MAGIC PETS STRAIGHT HERE.
THE PET FAIRIES SOON WILL SEE
THEIR SEVEN PETS LIVING WITH ME!

Shimmer and Misty are now safe and sound.

Now Kirsty and Rachel need to help

GEORGIA FIND HER GUINEA PIG, SPARKY.

Table of Contents

FARMYARD FUN   153

MAGIC IN MIDAIR!   163

GOBLINS UNDERCOVER   173

TRAPPED!   181

GIRLS AND GOBLINS AGREE   193

ODD ONE OUT   205

FARMYARD FUN

"This must be one of the cutest animals at Strawberry Farm!" Rachel Walker declared, her eyes shining. She stroked the woolly lamb in her arms. "It's so cuddly!"

"And hungry, too," her best friend, Kirsty Tate, added. She tilted up the bottle of milk she was using to feed the lamb, as a farmhand watched. "It almost finished this already!"

"Just watching it is making me thirsty!" Kirsty's mom said as the lamb drained the last few drops.

Rachel was staying with Kirsty's family for a week. This afternoon, they were having a great time at Strawberry Farm! They had already seen a flock of tiny ducklings heading out for their first swim on the pond. They took a pony ride on a sturdy little brown Shetland named Conker. And now they had the chance to hand-feed some of the lambs!

Rachel put the lamb down carefully, and both girls watched it teeter off to join the other lambs in the field.

"I saw a sign for Pet Corner over there," Rachel said, giving Kirsty a meaningful look. "Should we go there next?"

Kirsty smiled at her friend.

The two girls shared a wonderful secret: They'd been helping the Pet Fairies all week! Mean Jack Frost had kidnapped the Pet Fairies' seven magical pets, but the pets had managed to escape into the human world. Yesterday, Rachel and Kirsty had helped Bella the Bunny Fairy find her lost rabbit. And the day before, they'd reunited Katie the Kitten Fairy with her missing kitten. So Kirsty knew exactly what Rachel was hoping: maybe today they'd find another magical pet in the Pet Corner!

"That sounds great, but I think I'll grab a coffee while you two go ahead," Mrs. Tate said. "I'll meet you both back here at four o'clock."

"Sounds good," Kirsty replied, trying not to seem too enthusiastic. She loved her mom, but she and Rachel always had their very best adventures when they were alone! "See you later."

Mrs. Tate left for the coffee stand, and the two friends headed for Pet Corner.

"Here we are," Rachel said as they entered an area surrounded by a small fence. "Keep your eyes peeled for any magical pets!" she added in an excited whisper.

The girls began looking at all the rabbits and guinea pigs in the hutches. Every animal had a little sign outside its cage, telling visitors its name and favorite food.

"This rabbit is named Albie, and he likes carrot tops and brussel sprouts," Kirsty read aloud, peeking in at the fluffy gray rabbit. "Hello, Albie!"

"Rosie the guinea pig likes sunflower seeds and lettuce leaves," Rachel read on another hutch. "Millie, her sister, likes sliced apples. And Carrot, Rosie's baby, likes carrots . . . oh!"

Kirsty looked up. "What's wrong?" she asked.

Rachel was crouching down and peering into one of the hutches. "There are supposed to be three guinea pigs in here—Millie, Rosie, and baby Carrot," she told Kirsty. "But the baby guinea pig is missing!"

Kirsty hurried over. "Oh, no, look," she said. "The cage door is open—Carrot must have escaped!"

Out of the corner of her eye, Rachel spotted a flash of

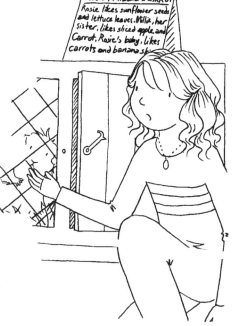

ROSIE, MILLIE & CARROT
Rosie likes sunflower seeds
and lettuce leaves. Millie, her
sister, likes sliced apple and
Carrot, Rosie's baby, likes
carrots and banana sl...

fur behind the hutches.
She turned to see a small
orange-and-white guinea
pig squeezing under the
wooden fence. "That
must be Carrot over
there!" she cried.

Kirsty shut the cage door firmly, then
jumped up to look. "Oh, no—he's heading
for the field of sheep!" she said, pointing.

Rachel ran off after the little guinea pig,
looking worried. "He's too young to be
out on his own," she said. "We have to
rescue him, Kirsty!"

MAGIC IN MIDAIR!

Kirsty and Rachel climbed over the wooden fence surrounding the field of sheep, and hurried after the guinea pig. Carrot was scampering toward a tree on the far side of the field. When the guinea pig reached the base of the tree, the little animal simply ran straight on up the trunk!

"I didn't think guinea pigs could do that!" Kirsty gasped. "I'll go after him, in case he gets stuck."

Kirsty clambered up into the tree, picking her way from branch to branch until she was within arm's reach of the little guinea pig. Carrot watched her curiously. "Hello," Kirsty said in a soft voice, reaching out toward him. As she did, the guinea pig twitched its nose and backed away playfully.

Kirsty stretched out her hand a little farther. "Come here, little Carrot," she said. Again the guinea pig backed away, and Kirsty thought she glimpsed a mischievous little smile on its face!

"I'm imagining things now," Kirsty said to herself. She inched farther along the branch and then leaned out, trying to reach the guinea pig. Just as her fingertips were about to touch Carrot's fur, he jumped right off the branch . . . and scampered away through the air!

Kirsty nearly fell out of the tree in surprise. "Rachel, look!" she cried excitedly, scrambling back down to the ground.

Rachel felt a thrill as she realized what was happening. "That's not Carrot, the farm guinea pig," she laughed. "It's Georgia the Guinea Pig Fairy's magic pet!" She and Kirsty had met all the Pet Fairies in Fairyland. "I wonder where Georgia is."

At that very moment, the girls heard the sound of cheerful singing above them. They looked up to see Georgia swooping toward them on the back of a blackbird!

"Georgia!" Rachel cried, waving at the pretty fairy.

Georgia waved back cheerfully as the blackbird perched above the girls on a tree branch. She had short black hair and wore a yellow top and suede skirt, both fringed with turquoise beads and tassels. She smiled as she slipped off the blackbird's back and thanked it for the ride. The blackbird sung a merry reply and fluttered away.

Georgia flew over to Rachel's shoulder. Her gauzy wings shimmered in the sunlight. "Hello, girls," she said, in a bright, friendly voice.

"We were looking for a lost guinea pig called Carrot," Kirsty explained eagerly. "But we found your magic pet instead, Georgia!"

Georgia twirled excitedly when she heard the good news. "I thought he was somewhere near here!" she declared, looking

around. "Oh, Sparky, hello!" she called, seeing the little orange-and-white guinea pig trotting along in midair. "I've missed you so much!"

Rachel smiled as
Sparky squeaked
happily to his fairy
owner and began
scampering toward her.

Georgia listened to
Sparky's eager squeaks.
"He says that he's been
looking for Carrot,
too," she told the girls. "And—"

But before Georgia could translate any
more of Sparky's message, one of the
sheep who'd been grazing nearby suddenly
stood up on its hind legs. To everybody's
amazement, the sheep had a butterfly
net. It swept the net through the air and
captured Sparky!

"Hey!" Kirsty cried. "What's going on?"

"That's not a sheep," Rachel called out in horror. A long green nose poked out from the creature's face. "It's a goblin in disguise!"

GOBLINS UNDERCOVER

A gleeful cackle floated through the air. The goblin ran across the field with Sparky trapped in the butterfly net.

"Oh, no!" Kirsty cried. "What are we going to do now?"

"I'll turn you into fairies so we can all fly after him," Georgia said quickly, waving her wand over the girls.

A stream of glittering turquoise sparkles swirled from the tip of her wand and whirled around Kirsty and Rachel. In an instant, both girls shrank down into tiny fairies.

Rachel fluttered her shimmering wings, feeling light as air as she floated off the ground. Being a fairy was the best thing in the whole world! But now, the girls had work to do! "Let's follow that sneaky goblin!" Rachel cried, zooming through the air after him.

"Don't worry, Sparky, we're coming!" Kirsty called out, following Rachel.

But as they flew over the field, several more sheep jumped up on their back legs and began swiping at Kirsty, Rachel, and Georgia with butterfly nets. There were more goblins in sheep disguises!

"Now they're chasing us!" Rachel warned, looking back over her shoulder. The goblins raced after them with nets in their hands and nasty grins on their faces.

"Fly higher," Georgia urged the girls. "Don't let them catch you, too!"

Kirsty, Rachel, and Georgia flew out of reach of the goblins. The goblin who had caught Sparky ran into a big, old barn and the girls zipped in after him.

It was very dark inside, and at first the three friends couldn't see very much in the gloom.

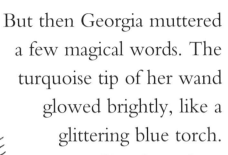

But then Georgia muttered
a few magical words. The
turquoise tip of her wand
glowed brightly, like a
glittering blue torch.
"Sparky, where
are you?" she
called softly,
fluttering over
to look behind
a stack of hay
bales. Kirsty and
Rachel were also
flying around the
barn, hoping to
catch a glimpse
of the guinea pig.

Suddenly, Sparky gave a couple of high-pitched squeaks. Kirsty, Rachel, and Georgia flew toward the sound at once. The magic pet's squeaks seemed to be coming from somewhere near the barn door.

Unfortunately, just as the girls and Georgia approached the door, the other goblins ran into the barn. They cackled with delight to see the three fairies, caught off-guard and hovering in front of them.

"Catch them!" one of the goblins urged, swinging his net around in an attempt to capture the fairies.

"Oh, no, you don't!" Georgia cried. She and the girls soared upward, away from the goblins.

Kirsty managed to dodge one goblin who made a grab for her, but the tallest one had her in his sights. Kirsty flew up just as the goblin swished his butterfly net down—she was trapped!

"Help!" she cried, beating her wings frantically.

"Ha!" the tall goblin smirked, putting a warty green hand over the top of the net. "You're my prisoner now!"

TRAPPED!

Georgia grabbed Rachel's hand. She pulled her up to a small, broken window above the barn door just as the goblins swung the door shut with a thump.

"What are we going to do?" Rachel asked Georgia. Her heart beat wildly as they squeezed through the hole in the window.

"The goblins are holding Kirsty prisoner!"

Georgia's eyes narrowed. "Don't worry, we'll free her," she vowed. "We just need to think of a way to rescue Kirsty and Sparky—fast!"

Rachel and Georgia fell silent as they thought about what to do. They could hear the goblins hooting triumphantly inside the barn.

"A guinea pig *and* a fairy," one of them crowed. "What a day!"

"Jack Frost is going to be happy with us today," another added smugly.

Then Rachel and Georgia heard
a scraping noise as the goblins slid
the bolt across the barn door, locking it.

"We'll sit tight until those two fairies
have gone," one goblin muttered.
"Then we'll take this fairy and the
guinea pig back to Jack Frost's castle."

Rachel thought it was horrible to hear
the goblins gloating.
She perched on
the window frame,
thinking hard.
"Georgia, do you
think Sparky might
be able to turn
himself into
an elephant and
knock the door
down?" she asked.

Georgia shook her head sadly. "Sparky won't be able to use any magic," she told Rachel. "None of the magic pets can use magic when they're afraid." She frowned concentrating. "We'll have to make the goblins leave the barn somehow," she went on. "Maybe we could tempt them out with something nice to eat?"

Rachel grinned as a brilliant idea suddenly popped into her head. "Or we could *scare* them out," she said eagerly. "Georgia, do you think you could use magic to create the sound of an angry bull?"

"Of course," Georgia replied. Then she grinned as she realized what Rachel had in mind. "Of course! The sound of an angry bull that has been woken by noisy goblins will be just the thing to drive them from the barn!" she whispered with a chuckle.

Rachel nodded happily. "The goblins will never know that it's only fairy magic they are hearing," she added.

Georgia and Rachel grinned at each other, then fluttered down to the ground.

"Let's give it a try," Georgia said. "The sooner we free Kirsty and Sparky, the sooner we can find little Carrot."

She waved her wand, sending more turquoise sparkles swirling around Rachel. In an instant, Rachel grew back to her usual size.

Then Georgia pointed her wand at the barn doors. They shimmered for a few seconds with magical turquoise light. "There," she whispered to Rachel. "I've used magic to hold the doors shut. Even if the goblins unbolt them, they won't be able to come out until we let them."

Rachel smiled. "And we'll only let them out when they promise to hand over Kirsty and Sparky," she whispered back. "It's a great idea, Georgia!" Then, with a wink at the smiling fairy, Rachel raised her voice. "Beware of the bull?" she said, as if she were reading aloud from a sign. "I wonder if those goblins know they're stuck in the barn with Farmer Tom's mean old bull? Phew! It's got a bad temper—it's way too crazy to be out in the fields." She laughed loudly. "I wouldn't want to be in there when the bull wakes up!"

Rachel glanced up at Georgia, who was hovering outside the window above the barn door. With a wave of her wand, the little fairy sent a stream of magic all the way into the darkest corner of the barn.

Snort! Grunt! CRASH! A terrible commotion started where Georgia's magic had landed. There was a thunderous, hoof-stamping sound.

Georgia flew back down to perch on Rachel's shoulder. She tried not to laugh out loud at their clever trick.

Rachel pressed her ear to the barn door to listen to the goblins.

"Whose stupid idea was it to come in here, anyway?" one of them hissed nervously.

"Farmer Tom's crazy b-b-bull sounds really a-a-angry!" another goblin stuttered.

Rachel and Georgia heard the sound of the bolt being pulled back. Then one of the goblins tried to push the door open, but, of course, Georgia's magic held the door firmly shut.

"You're trapped in there," Rachel called, "with Farmer Tom's crazy bull!"

"Maybe the bull will make a nice pet for Jack Frost," Georgia suggested sweetly.

"Hey, let us out right now!" a goblin demanded, thumping on the door.

"I don't think so," Georgia replied in her silvery fairy voice. Then she zoomed up to the

window and waved her
wand again, sending
more magic into the
barn. Immediately, the
roar of an angry bull
started up again, but
this time it sounded
even louder!

"Oh, all that shouting
seems to have made the bull even angrier!"
Georgia remarked.

The goblins hammered on the door in
panic. "Let us out right now!" they cried.

GIRLS AND GOBLINS AGREE

"You let Kirsty and Sparky go, and then we'll let you out of the barn!" Rachel shouted to the goblins.

There was a minute of silence. "We can't tell Jack Frost that we've let another of those pesky pets slip through our fingers," Rachel heard one goblin whisper. "First we messed up the kitten kidnap, then the bunny bagging. If we come back today without the guinea pig—"

"We *can't* go back without the guinea pig," another goblin interrupted. "But how about if we . . ."

Rachel pressed her ear as close to the barn door as possible, but the goblins were talking so quietly now that she couldn't hear what they were plotting.

"The fairy can go, but the guinea pig's staying with us!" a goblin voice announced after a moment.

Rachel looked at Georgia sadly. She hadn't been expecting that response! "What do we say?" she whispered.

"Let's agree, and then at least we'll know Kirsty's safe," Georgia replied. "Maybe one of you will be able to grab Sparky as the goblins come out of the barn."

Rachel nodded. "OK," she said reluctantly. Then she turned back to the barn door.

"It's a deal," she shouted to the goblins. "Set Kirsty free!"

A moment passed while Rachel and Georgia waited to see if the goblins were plotting a trick of their own. Then Kirsty zoomed out of the window and flew down to join them, smiling with relief.

Georgia waved her wand and turned Kirsty back into a girl.

Rachel
hugged her
tightly. "Are
you all right?
Were they
mean to you
and Sparky?"
she asked.

"I'm fine,"
Kirsty said.
"And so is
Sparky. He's
being very
quiet, but he
isn't hurt."

A loud knocking came from the other
side of the barn door. "A deal's
a deal," one of the goblins yelled. "Open
up before this crazy bull finds us."

Georgia pointed her wand at the doors.

"We're going to try and grab the goblin who has Sparky, OK?" Rachel whispered to Kirsty.

Kirsty nodded. "He was standing behind the others, at the back," she told Rachel quietly. "Ready when you are, Georgia."

Georgia waved her wand. The barn doors glittered with bright blue light again, then burst open. The goblins immediately raced out of the barn.

"Quick! Before the bull starts chasing us!" one of them shrieked.

Kirsty and Rachel lunged for the last goblin, who was clutching Sparky. Their hands closed around empty air as he nimbly dodged them and sprinted away across the field.

"He's getting away!" cried Rachel.

Kirsty looked around frantically for something she could use to stop the goblin.

Suddenly, she spotted an old rope just inside the barn. "Georgia, could you use magic to turn that rope into a lasso for me?" she asked quickly.

"Yes," the fairy replied, waving her wand. Turquoise fairy dust spiralled through the air. The frayed old rope turned into a lasso and flew straight up into Kirsty's hand.

Kirsty swung the loop of the lasso around her head, keeping her eyes fixed on the goblin who was running off with Sparky. Then she launched the lasso straight at him.

The girls held their breath as the lasso flew through the air. It seemed to be heading in the wrong direction, but Georgia quickly pointed her wand at it. The lasso shone with blue magic and veered back on course, toward the goblin. The loop of rope fell right over his head and caught tight around his middle, pinning his arms by his sides.

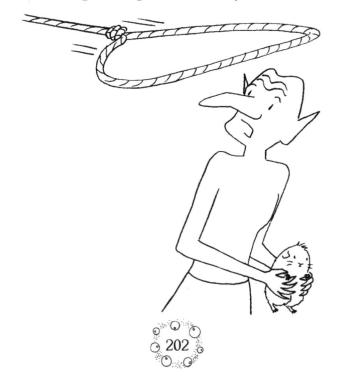

The goblin tried to keep running, but the
rope pulled itself magically out of Kirsty's
hands and wound itself around the goblin
until he had to stop.

"Got him!" Kirsty cheered triumphantly.

ODD ONE OUT

"Help!" the lassoed goblin yelled to his friends, but they were too busy running away from the imaginary bull to notice.

Rachel and Kirsty walked calmly over to the struggling goblin. Sparky, who was still in the goblin's hands, squeaked hello.

"Come here, Sparky," Rachel said, gently lifting him out of the goblin's fingers.

Sparky squeaked even louder when he saw Georgia fluttering in midair. With a twitch of his nose, he jumped up toward her. As he leaped through the air, he shrank to his usual tiny size. Georgia picked him up happily and gave him a big hug.

"Hey! What about me?" the goblin shouted angrily, still tangled in the rope.

Georgia smiled at him. "Don't worry, the magic will wear off the rope soon," she assured him. "In a couple of hours or so, you'll be free . . ."

"A couple of hours?" the goblin groaned.

Georgia winked at Kirsty and Rachel as they began making their way back toward Pet Corner. "It will only be a couple of minutes, really," she whispered with a laugh.

Sparky started squeaking urgently, and suddenly Georgia looked worried. "Of course!" she cried. "We have to find poor little Carrot! I'd almost forgotten about him."

Rachel looked at her watch. "It's a quarter to four already," she said. "Kirsty, we have to meet your mom in fifteen minutes. We don't have much time to look for Carrot."

"Then I'll turn you back into fairies," Georgia said, waving her wand briskly. "That way we can all fly around and look for him. Let's split up and meet back at Carrot's hutch in five minutes."

Rachel and Kirsty zoomed off in different directions, searching for the little, lost guinea pig. Kirsty checked out the play area, the cow barn, and even popped through the windows of the gift shop. Rachel hunted around the pig pen, the duck pond, and the stables. There was no sign of Carrot anywhere.

"I don't understand it," Georgia said when they met up with her again five minutes later. "Where could he be?"

"We should go soon," Rachel said sadly, "but I can't leave the farm without knowing that Carrot's safe!"

Kirsty suddenly pointed ahead to where a mother hen was being followed by a line of her chicks. "Wait a minute," she said, narrowing her eyes. "That's a strange-looking looking chick at the end of the line!"

Rachel looked where Kirsty was pointing, and then giggled in relief. The last "chick" in the line was not yellow and fluffy, like the others. It was a small, carrot-colored guinea pig!

"Carrot's adopted a new family," Georgia chuckled. "How sweet!"

Sparky scampered over to Carrot
and squeaked at him happily. Georgia,
Rachel, and Kirsty watched as Carrot
looked at Sparky, then back at the chicks,
as if he was figuring something out.
Then he rubbed noses with Sparky and
squeaked.

Georgia grinned. "He says he's enjoyed
being part of the hen family, but he's
ready to go home now," she translated.
"And we're ready too, little Carrot!"

Georgia checked to make sure that nobody else was in sight. Then she waved her wand over Rachel and Kirsty, turning them back into girls. Kirsty went over and picked up Carrot. "Come on," she said gently.  "Let's take you back to your hutch."

As soon as Kirsty had placed Carrot back in his hutch, Rosie and Millie, Carrot's mom and aunt, rushed over and squeaked at Carrot excitedly. Then all three of them rubbed noses, and Carrot nestled against Rosie, looking very happy.

Georgia waved her wand to make sure that the cage door was tightly shut. "There will be no more going back to the hen house, OK?" she said to Carrot, with a smile.

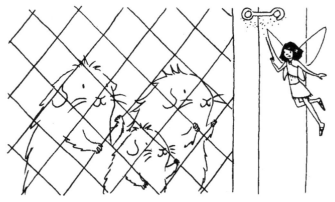

Then she picked up Sparky and turned to the girls. "It's almost four o'clock. You'd better go," she told them. "And we should fly back to Fairyland, Sparky—where I'm going to make sure Jack Frost never gets anywhere near you again!"

Sparky nuzzled Georgia's arm and she pet him gently. "Thank you for everything," she said to Kirsty and Rachel. "Sparky says thank you, too."

Kirsty and Rachel hugged the tiny fairy good-bye, and gave Sparky a gentle scratch. Sparky squeaked good-bye to the girls, then squeaked in the direction of Carrot's cage. A bunch of squeaks came back in reply, as if the farm guinea pigs were calling out their good-byes too.

And then, with
a burst of
turquoise sparkles
that glittered in
the afternoon
sunlight, Georgia
and Sparky vanished.

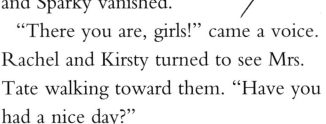

"There you are, girls!" came a voice.
Rachel and Kirsty turned to see Mrs.
Tate walking toward them. "Have you
had a nice day?"

"Great, thanks,
Mom," Kirsty replied
with a smile. "Wasn't
it, Rachel?"

"Oh, yes," Rachel
agreed. She grinned
as she noticed a pot
of sunflower seeds,

some sliced apples, and a whole pile of
carrot sticks in the guinea pigs' cage. She
was sure that the food was a gift from
Georgia! It definitely hadn't been there
before. "Today's been magic!" Rachel
said, sighing happily.

LAUREN
THE PUPPY FAIRY

FAIRIES WITH THEIR PETS I SEE
AND YET NO PET HAS CHOSEN ME!
SO I WILL GET SOME OF MY OWN
TO SHARE MY PERFECT FROSTY HOME.

THIS SPELL I CAST, ITS AIM IS CLEAR:
TO BRING THE MAGIC PETS STRAIGHT HERE.
THE PET FAIRIES SOON WILL SEE
THEIR SEVEN PETS LIVING WITH ME!

Shimmer, Misty, and Sparky have been returned to their

fairies. Now Kirsty and Rachel need to help

LAUREN FIND HER PUPPY, SUNNY.

Table of Contents

PUPPIES ON SHOW   223

PUPPY, COME BACK!   237

TROUBLE SCOOTS UP   247

GRABBED BY GOBLINS!   257

NEW FRIENDS   267

PUPPY LOVE   281

PUPPIES ON SHOW

"Look at that zucchini, Kirsty," Rachel Walker laughed, pointing at the giant green vegetable on the display table. "It's almost as big as I am!"

Kirsty Tate read the card propped in front of the zucchini. "It won a prize," she announced. "It's the biggest vegetable at the Wetherbury Spring Show."

There were other enormous vegetables on the table. The girls stared at the giant-size carrots and onions. There were also huge bowls of daffodils, tulips, and bluebells. The best flower displays had won prizes, too.

"This is great!" Rachel declared. "I wish we had a Spring Show back home."

Rachel was staying in Wetherbury
with Kirsty for the week, and the girls
had spent the whole afternoon at the
show. The field was crammed with
booths selling homemade cakes, cookies,
and jams, and there were pony rides
and a huge red-and-yellow bouncy
castle. Rachel and Kirsty were having a
great time!

"I think we've been around the whole
show," Kirsty said at last. "Mom and Dad
will be here to pick us up soon."

"Should we have one last look at our
favorite stall?" Rachel asked eagerly.

"You mean the one for Wetherbury
Animal Shelter?" Kirsty said with a smile.

Rachel nodded. "I want to see if they've
found homes for those four puppies."

"I hope so," Kirsty said. "They were really cute! And speaking of pets . . ." She lowered her voice so that she wouldn't be overheard. "Do you think we might find another fairy pet today?"

"We'll just have to keep our eyes open!" Rachel whispered in a determined voice.

No one else knew Kirsty and Rachel's wonderful secret. They were friends with the fairies!

Whenever there was trouble in Fairyland, the girls were always happy to help. Mean Jack Frost caused lots of problems for the fairies. This time, he had stolen the seven Pet Fairies' magical animals! But the mischievous pets had escaped from Jack Frost, and were now lost in the human world. Rachel and Kirsty were trying to find the pets and return them to their fairy owners before Jack Frost's goblins caught them!

"It's too bad Jack Frost can't get his own pet, instead of trying to steal someone else's!" Kirsty remarked.

"Yes, but remember what the fairies told us," Rachel reminded her. "In Fairyland, the pets choose their owners—and none of them has ever chosen Jack Frost!"

"There must be the perfect pet for him somewhere," Kirsty said thoughtfully. "But it would have to be mean, just like him!"

The girls headed toward the animal shelter booth. But as they got closer, Rachel's face fell. "Look, Kirsty," she said sadly. "There's still one puppy left."

Next to the booth was a large, fenced-in pen. When the girls had been there before, there had been four puppies in it—one brown, one white, and two black-and-white ones.

Now only one black-and-white puppy remained. It was sitting in a corner, chewing on a piece of rope.

"Oh, poor pup!" Kirsty said, sighing. She bent over the pen. The puppy immediately dropped the rope and bounced over, its tail wagging furiously. "It looks lonely."

Mr. Gregory, the vet who ran the animal shelter, was taking down the posters pinned up on the booth. Kirsty smiled at him. She knew him because she'd taken her kitten, Pearl, to Mr. Gregory to get her shots.

"Hello," Mr. Gregory said, smiling back. "It's Kirsty Tate, isn't it? How's Pearl?"

Kirsty grinned. "She's great, thanks!" she replied. "What's the puppy's name, Mr. Gregory?"

"I call him Bouncer," the vet replied, "but it'll be up to his new owners to give him his real name."

The puppy was licking Kirsty's fingers through the wire fence. Bouncer looked so adorable that the girls just couldn't understand why no one had given him a home yet!

"Do you need any help packing up?" Rachel asked Mr. Gregory as he began clearing pamphlets from the table.

"That's very kind of you," Mr. Gregory said gratefully. "Would you mind taking Bouncer for a quick walk around the grounds? He's been cooped up in that pen all day."

Rachel and Kirsty looked at each other in excitement. "We'd love to!" they chorused.

Mr. Gregory took a leash from his pocket and opened the pen. Bouncer was very excited when he saw the leash. He jumped around, giving little yaps of joy as the vet attached the leash to his collar.

"You walk him first," Rachel said to Kirsty. Kirsty took the leash and they set off, with the puppy running along beside them.

"Don't be too long, girls," Mr. Gregory called. "It'll only take me half an hour to pack up."

"OK," Rachel replied with a wave.

Bouncer pulled excitedly at the leash, sniffing here and there, as the girls walked between the booths. Everyone else was starting to pack up, too. There were still a few children left on the bouncy castle, but their parents were doing their best to convince them to come down so that it could be deflated.

"I think Bouncer's going to pull my arm off!" Kirsty laughed as the puppy strained to go faster. "He's so excited."

"That's because he just spotted another dog," Rachel said, pointing ahead.

A brown-and-white puppy with a shaggy coat and long, floppy ears had seen them, too. It came bounding down the hill toward them.

"Isn't it cute?" Kirsty laughed as the pup drew nearer, waving his tail in greeting. "He's a springer spaniel, I think."

Bouncer was dancing around the girls' legs, bursting with excitement at the sight of his new puppy friend. The spaniel ran up to them, gave a little yap, and dashed off again.

Bouncer hurtled after him and both girls' eyes widened in horror as they realized that the leash was now hanging loosely in Kirsty's hand. Somehow, Bouncer had gotten free!

"Oh, no!" Rachel gasped. "How did that happen?"

"I don't know," Kirsty replied, anxiously. "But we'd better get him back right away!"

PUPPY, COME BACK!

Rachel and Kirsty ran after the excited puppy.

"I'm sure the leash was attached to Bouncer's collar correctly, Rachel," Kirsty panted. "There's something very strange going on here."

"I think you're right," Rachel agreed as she caught up with the puppies.

The two dogs had stopped chasing each other. Now they were running around in circles, snapping playfully at each other's tails.

Kirsty looked around. "At least they're safe here," she pointed out. The puppies were in a corner of the grounds, not far from the high fence that separated the field from the road. "They can't get out onto the street."

"I wonder where the spaniel's owner is," Rachel said, sounding worried. "I don't see anyone nearby."

"I think there's a name tag on its collar," Kirsty said. She bent over the two puppies, who were rolling around on the grass. "Look, Rachel."

The girls stared closely at the spaniel's blue collar. A name tag in the shape of a little silver bone hung from it. SUNNY was written in glittering blue letters.

"Hello, Sunny," said Kirsty.

The spaniel licked Kirsty's hand and stared up at her with big brown eyes.

"There's no phone number or address," Rachel said, taking a closer look at the name tag.

"Let's tell Mr. Gregory when we take Bouncer back," Kirsty suggested. "He'll know what to do."

"Good idea," agreed Rachel.

Tail wagging, Sunny jumped to his feet and gave a happy little yap. But then, to Rachel and Kirsty's amazement, a sparkly, red rubber ball appeared in midair and fell

to the ground! The spaniel pounced on it and then nudged it toward Bouncer.

"Did you see that, Kirsty?" Rachel gasped. "Or did I imagine it?"

"I saw a ball appear from thin air, if that's what you mean!" Kirsty replied, her voice shaking with excitement. The two dogs were playing with the ball now, knocking it back and forth. "Rachel, do you think Sunny could be one of the magic fairy pets?"

Rachel stared at the spaniel. He was standing with his head tilted to one side, watching Bouncer. "Yes, I think he might be," she agreed.

Bouncer dropped the ball to bark at Sunny. The ball landed on the grassy hill and began to roll away from the puppy, gathering speed. It was heading straight toward an open gate that led out onto the busy road. To the girls' horror, Bouncer suddenly turned and raced after it.

"Bouncer!" Rachel yelled, as the puppy headed for the gate. "Kirsty, we have to stop him!"

With Sunny at their heels, the girls chased after the puppy, calling his name.

But Bouncer was too intent on catching the ball to notice.

"We're too far away to catch him," Kirsty cried. "Bouncer, stop!"

But no sooner were the words out of Kirsty's mouth, than Sunny raced ahead of the girls and gave another little yap. Rachel blinked as she spotted a faint shimmer of silver fairy dust around Sunny. The next moment, a big, meaty bone appeared in Bouncer's path.

The puppy skidded to a halt, ignoring the ball as it bounced out of the gate and onto the road. He was far more interested in the juicy bone! With a little yelp of delight, Bouncer lay down to have a good chew.

"That was close!" Kirsty panted, bending down to clip Bouncer's leash on again.

"Yes, that bone turned up just in time," Rachel agreed, patting Sunny. "You know, Kirsty, I think Bouncer getting off his leash, and then the ball and the bone appearing out of nowhere, can only mean one thing . . ."

Kirsty nodded seriously. "Sunny must be Lauren the Puppy Fairy's missing pet!" she declared.

TROUBLE SCOOTS UP

"He is!" laughed a light, silvery voice above the girls' heads.

Rachel and Kirsty glanced up. A pink balloon was floating down toward them. Holding onto the string, waving and smiling at them, was Lauren the Puppy Fairy.

"Hello," Kirsty and Rachel called, beaming happily. Sunny had spotted his owner, too, and was jumping around excitedly.

Lauren floated down toward them, her long light brown hair trailing in the breeze. She wore pink cargo pants, a cropped pink top, and sneakers. Waving her wand at the girls, she fluttered down to stand on Sunny's back.

"I'm so glad to see you, Sunny!" Lauren cried happily, dropping a tiny kiss on top of her pet's head. "And you too, girls."

"We're so glad you're here!" Kirsty replied.

"I think Sunny's tail is going to fall off if he doesn't stop wagging it so hard!" Rachel laughed.

The spaniel gave a happy bark, turning its shaggy head to look lovingly at its owner. Wondering what was going on, Bouncer looked up from his bone and trotted over to join them. He sniffed curiously at Lauren, and she put out her little hand to stroke his nose.

"I knew Sunny was around here somewhere," Lauren told the girls. "I'm so glad you found him!"

Rachel and Kirsty smiled.

"Actually, he found us!" Rachel said.

"Well, he found Bouncer," added Kirsty. "We've been lucky today, though. We haven't seen any goblins!"

"Yes, this was the easiest pet rescue so far," Rachel agreed.

"Ha, ha, ha!" The sound of cruel giggling behind them made Kirsty, Rachel, Lauren, and even the puppies jump. Goblins!

A shiny silver scooter was speeding along the path toward them. It was crowded with goblins! Two of them were using their feet to propel the scooter along as fast as they could. Three others were balanced on their shoulders, wobbling back and forth as the scooter zoomed along.

The girls and Lauren were taken by surprise! Before they could do anything, the scooter had crashed to a stop in front of them. The goblins tumbled off in a heap. One rolled toward Sunny, and another toward Bouncer.

"*Oof!*" Lauren gasped as the first goblin pushed her off Sunny's back, then snatched up the puppy.

"Is this the magic puppy?" the goblin yelled to the others.

"Don't know!" they shouted back, looking from Sunny to Bouncer.

"Grab both!"

The first goblin leaped back on the scooter, still clutching Sunny.

"Put him down!" Lauren yelled angrily, scrambling to her feet.

"Give him back!" shouted Rachel, as the second goblin grabbed Bouncer, yanked the leash from Kirsty's hand, and then jumped onto the scooter.

"Catch us if you can!" jeered the goblins, whizzing away down the hill. The girls and Lauren watched as the scooter sped off, both puppies whimpering in fear.

"Jack Frost is going to be very pleased with us when he sees the magic puppy," one of the goblins shouted.

"Hooray!" cheered his goblin friends.

GRABBED BY GOBLINS!

"We have to go after them!" Lauren
declared, her face pale. "It will be quicker
if I turn you into fairies, girls."

Kirsty and Rachel nodded. Hearts
thumping, they waited as Lauren waved
her wand and showered them with
sparkling pink fairy dust.

As soon as they were fairy-size, the girls fluttered up into the air to join their friend and chase down the goblins. But the goblins had a head start and were whizzing farther and farther away every second.

"They're getting away!" Rachel gasped.

The goblins were heading in the direction of the bouncy castle. Rachel, Kirsty, and

Lauren could see that all the children had left the castle, and it was slowly being deflated. Meanwhile, one of the goblins had climbed up onto the handlebars and was yelling instructions at the others.

"Turn left! No, not that way!" he roared furiously.

The other goblins weren't paying attention. They were struggling to hold the wriggling puppies, and arguing loudly at the same time.

"Not that way—this way!"

"No, that's not right!"

One of the goblins grabbed the handlebars and tried to yank them in the opposite direction. The goblin who was perched there almost fell off! But the scooter still zoomed down the hill, pulling even farther away from Lauren, Rachel, and Kirsty.

"Faster, girls!" Lauren called. "We must stop them!"

Kirsty frowned. The goblins were so far ahead, it seemed almost impossible to catch up with them! Her gaze fell on the slowly deflating bouncy castle, and that gave her an idea . . .

"Lauren!" Kirsty cried breathlessly. "Bouncer and Sunny are only puppies, but aren't the goblins scared of big dogs? I remember they  were scared of Buttons, Rachel's dog."

Lauren nodded.

"Well, could you make a really big dog appear in front of the scooter?" Kirsty went on. "Maybe we can force the goblins to swerve and crash into the bouncy castle. That would slow them down!"

"Great idea, Kirsty!" Rachel said eagerly. Lauren was already lifting her wand.

As the girls watched, a shower of glittery pink sparkles whooshed from the tip of Lauren's wand toward the goblins. There was a puff of pink smoke, and just to the left of the scooter, a German shepherd appeared out of thin air. Rachel and Kirsty stared at it in surprise. This was no ordinary German shepherd. It was black with white stripes, just like a zebra!

"*Woof! Woof! Woof!*" the dog barked loudly.

The goblins screeched with fear.

"A big, scary dog!" the one sitting on the handlebars yelled. "Quick, get away!"

All the goblins grabbed the handlebars and wrenched them to the right. Immediately, the scooter careened away from the dog, straight toward the bouncy castle.

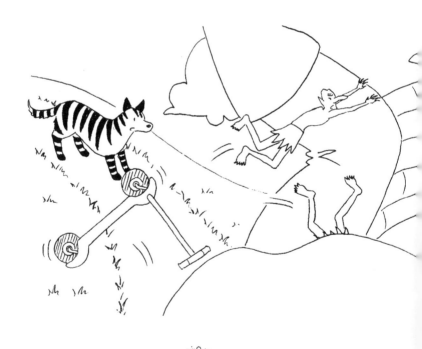

"No!" shouted the goblin on the handlebars. "We're going to crash!"

But he was too late. As Lauren, Rachel, and Kirsty watched, the scooter hit the bouncy castle. The goblins went flying! The puppies barked and the goblins shrieked with anger, but they all landed safely on the castle, disappearing into its folds.

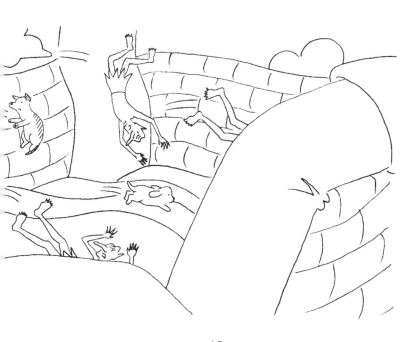

Quickly, Lauren waved her wand to make the German shepherd disappear. Then she, Rachel, and Kirsty flew over to the bouncy castle.

"It's a good thing there's hardly anyone around!" Kirsty said, looking relieved.

"Yes, but what about the man who's packing the bouncy castle?" Rachel asked. "He's sure to come back soon. How are we going to get the puppies and the goblins out of there?"

NEW FRIENDS

Lauren, Kirsty, and Rachel hovered over the bouncy castle, wondering what to do. Then, to their relief, they suddenly heard a tiny bark.

A moment later, Sunny's head popped up. He wriggled out of the castle, barking with delight as he spotted Lauren. Bouncer followed him, and together they bounced toward the edge of the half-deflated castle, enjoying this new game.

"Sunny!" Lauren called, holding her arms open.

Rachel and Kirsty saw a shimmer of glittering magic around the spaniel as it shrank to fairy-pet size. Then he jumped off the bouncy castle and bounded magically through the air toward Lauren.

"It's OK, Bouncer," laughed Rachel, seeing the puppy stare at Sunny in surprise. "It's fairy magic!"

"Don't you try it, though!" Kirsty added with a laugh.

Sunny had run straight into Lauren's arms, and was now licking her nose gently. Laughing, Lauren raised her wand. In three sparkling seconds, Rachel and Kirsty were back to their normal size.

Bouncer blinked. Then he jumped down from the castle and dashed joyfully over to Rachel and Kirsty. Rachel picked up his leash and held it tightly, as she bent down to pet him.

"What's Bouncer looking at?" asked Kirsty, noticing that the little puppy was peering curiously at something behind them.

Rachel turned to see. "Here comes the bouncy castle man!" she whispered. "Lauren—you and Sunny had better hide!"

Lauren nodded. Still holding Sunny, she zoomed down to hide in Rachel's pocket.

The bouncy castle operator was a young man with a friendly face. He smiled at Kirsty and Rachel. "Hi," he said, "Did you enjoy the Spring show?"

"It was great," Kirsty replied, and Rachel nodded.

The bouncy castle operator glanced down at Bouncer, who was sniffing eagerly at the man's legs.

"What a cute puppy!" he said, bending down to scratch Bouncer's head. "My daughter, Annie, would love a dog like this."

"How old is Annie?" asked Rachel.

"She'll be six next week," the man replied. "Actually, her mom and I are planning on getting her a puppy for her birthday. Excuse me," he went on, "I have to get this castle put away."

Whistling to himself, the man went around the back of the bouncy castle, where all the cables were hidden.

"What are we going to do?" Rachel whispered, as Lauren and Sunny popped their heads out of her pocket. "He's not going to be very happy when he finds a bunch of angry goblins in his castle."

But Kirsty was shaking her head and laughing. "Look!" She pointed at the front of the castle. "He won't see them because they're coming out this side. And it's the goblins who don't look very happy!"

The goblins were finally emerging from beneath the folds of rubber. They were grumbling and groaning and blaming one another as usual. Two of them were dragging the silver scooter along. Complaining loudly, they all jumped to the ground and stalked off, pulling the scooter behind them.

"That was all your fault!"

"I told you we were going to crash!"

"And now we've lost the magic puppy. Who's going to tell Jack Frost?"

Kirsty, Rachel, and Lauren couldn't help laughing.

"Daddy! Daddy, where are you?" came a voice.

Immediately, Lauren ducked out of sight and the girls turned to see who was coming.

A girl with dark curly hair and big blue eyes was running toward them. "Daddy, where are you?" she called again.

"Around the back of the castle, sweetheart," the man yelled back.

"That must be Annie," Kirsty whispered.

Just then, Annie caught sight of Bouncer. Her face broke into a huge smile and she dashed straight toward him. "What a sweet puppy!" she said, kneeling down to hug him. Bouncer yapped a greeting and licked her cheek, his tail wagging furiously. "Oh, I wish I had a puppy like you!"

"Would you like to hold his leash?" Rachel asked, offering it to her.

Annie's eyes lit up. "Can I really?" she gasped. "Oh, thank you!"

She took the leash, and the girls watched as Annie led Bouncer on a little walk in front of the castle. Bouncer bounded alongside her, obviously enjoying himself. Then he spied the untied shoelace of one of Annie's sneakers, and pounced on it, grabbing it in his teeth.

Annie laughed and crouched down to tug the lace gently. Kirsty and Rachel smiled as Bouncer held on to it, enjoying the game.

Suddenly, Kirsty nudged Rachel.
"Look, Rachel!" she whispered,
her voice full of excitement. "There's
a magical sparkle all around Annie
and Bouncer!"

PUPPY LOVE

Rachel stared at the little girl and the puppy. Kirsty was right! A shimmery haze hung in the air around them.

"Fairy magic!" Rachel whispered back. "Bouncer's meant to be with Annie. She's the owner he's been waiting for!"

At that moment, the man came out from behind the bouncy castle, which was now almost fully deflated. He smiled as he saw Annie and Bouncer playing together.

"That's really a great puppy, girls," he said with a smile. "Which one of you is the owner?"

Rachel saw her chance. "The puppy's not mine or Kirsty's," she explained. "It's from the animal shelter booth. Its brothers and sisters have all been adopted today, and it's the only one left."

"Oh, really?" The man frowned.

"I didn't see the animal shelter booth."

Annie had been listening to their conversation, her eyes wide. Now she tugged at her dad's sleeve. "Daddy!" she cried. "This poor little puppy doesn't have a home!"

Rachel and Kirsty held their breath as they waited for Annie's dad to reply. He looked at the eager face of his little girl and then down into Bouncer's brown eyes.

"Well . . ." he began, "I'll finish up here, and then we'll go over to the animal shelter booth. But don't get your hopes up too much, Annie. Someone else may want to adopt that dog."

"Oh, thank you, Daddy!" Annie gasped joyfully, throwing her arms around him. Rachel and Kirsty beamed at each other. Even Bouncer seemed to know that something exciting was going on, because he gave two happy barks.

The man disappeared behind the castle to finish his work, and Annie and Bouncer went with him.

"Good job, girls!" Lauren said, flying out of Rachel's pocket. Sunny followed her, bounding through the air to perch on Kirsty's shoulder. "Annie is the puppy's perfect owner!"

"Everything's worked out perfectly," Rachel said, and Kirsty nodded.

"I don't know how I can ever thank

you," Lauren went on gratefully. "Without you, I wouldn't have gotten Sunny back."

"*Woof*!" Sunny agreed, rubbing his tiny black nose against Kirsty's cheek.

"But we must go home to Fairyland now," Lauren said, raising her wand. "Everyone will be anxious to find out if I have gotten my magic pet back. Say good-bye, Sunny."

Sunny gave a little yap, wagging his tail so hard it tickled Kirsty's ear. Then he ran over to Lauren, who waved her wand so that a shower of sparkling fairy dust fell around them.

"Oh!" Lauren called, "I almost forgot! Say good-bye to Barney for me!"

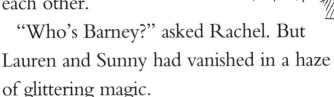

Confused, Rachel and Kirsty looked at each other.

"Who's Barney?" asked Rachel. But Lauren and Sunny had vanished in a haze of glittering magic.

A moment later, Annie, Bouncer, and Annie's dad walked up.

"Daddy, we'll have to give my new puppy a name," Annie was saying. "Can I call him Barney?"

Her dad smiled. "We need to talk to the people at the animal shelter before we make any plans," he said. "But if it's OK for us to adopt him, then we'll call him Barney."

Rachel and Kirsty grinned at each other, as they followed Annie and her father toward the animal shelter booth.

"So *that's* why Lauren told us to say good-bye to Barney!" Kirsty whispered. "Mr. Gregory's going to be really happy that Barney's found a home at last."

The two girls beamed as they watched Annie's father chatting with Mr. Gregory. The vet was nodding and smiling, while Annie and Barney were chasing each other across the grass.

"Everyone in Fairyland is going to be happy that Sunny's safely home again, too!" Rachel added.

Kirsty nodded. "I love happy endings!" she said, sighing.

Now it's time for Kirsty and
Rachel to help . . .

HARRIET the HAMSTER FAIRY.

Read on for a sneak peek . . .

HARRIET
THE HAMSTER FAIRY

HAMSTER-SITTING

"Here we go," Kirsty Tate said to her best friend, Rachel Walker. She turned the key in the back door of her neighbors' house. "Nibbles! Time for breakfast!" she called, as the door swung open. "Just wait until you see him," she said to Rachel with a grin. "He's adorable. I love hamster-sitting!"

Kirsty's neighbor, Jamie Cooper, had asked Kirsty to feed Nibbles, his little orange-and-white hamster, while he and his parents were on vacation. She had said yes right away!

"We just need to fill up his food and water dishes," Kirsty told Rachel. "And if we're lucky, he might eat his sunflower seeds out of our hands!"

"How cute!" Rachel said. "Where's his cage?"

"Over here," Kirsty replied, heading into the living room.

Excitement bubbled up inside Rachel as she followed her friend. They were going to see another pet after all. Over the last few days, she and Kirsty had shared some amazing pet adventures!

Rachel was staying with Kirsty's family for a whole week. On the very first day of her visit, the two girls had met the Pet Fairies! The fairies had asked Rachel and Kirsty for their help. Jack Frost had wanted a pet of his own, but in Fairyland, pets choose their owners. None of them had chosen Jack Frost! He had been so annoyed that he had stolen the Pet Fairies' magical pets.

Luckily, the pets had all escaped from
Jack Frost into the human world. But
now they were lost!

Rachel and Kirsty were determined
to help the Pet Fairies find the magic
pets before Jack Frost's goblins did. So
far, the girls had found four: Shimmer
the kitten, Misty the bunny, Sparky the
guinea pig, and Sunny the puppy. But
there were still three pets missing!

Kirsty led Rachel across the living
room to the side table where Nibbles's
cage stood. But when the girls arrived,
they saw at once that something was
wrong: the cage door was wide open!

"Oh, no!" Kirsty cried. "Don't
tell me that Nibbles escaped on my
very first day of watching him!" She
carefully put her hand into the cage and

searched through the wood shavings and shredded newspaper for the little hamster, but it was too late. The cage was empty.

Kirsty and Rachel began searching everywhere they could think of. They looked under the table, around all the chairs, and behind the television. But there was no sign of Jamie's hamster.

"Nibbles!" Rachel called, picking up the hamster's food and rattling it. "Nibbles, come have something to eat."

"Jamie's going to be so upset if he comes home and Nibbles is missing," Kirsty said. "Nibbles! Where are you?"

"He could be anywhere in the house," Rachel said. "Come on, let's try another room."

Kirsty nodded, and the girls headed out of the living room. But just as they reached the door, Kirsty spotted something.

"Rachel, look!" she cried, bending down to examine the carpet.

She picked up a stray wood shaving and held it up for her friend to see. "A clue!"

"It must have been stuck to one of Nibbles's feet when he climbed out of the cage," Rachel guessed. "Look, there's another one by the doorway. And another!"

The two girls followed the trail of wood shavings out into the hall. There, they began searching around the coat rack and the side table.

Kirsty picked up the mail from the doormat and noticed that some of the envelopes were a little shredded. "Look!" she exclaimed. "Someone's been tearing up the mail!" Then she smiled as she realized what had happened. "Hamsters shred paper to make nests, don't they?" she asked. "I think Nibbles must have started trying to make a nest here!" She giggled as she put the letters on the table. "Where did he go next, I wonder?"

RAINBOW magic

More Titles to Read

RAINBOW FAIRIES 1-4

RAINBOW FAIRIES 5-7
+ BONUS PET FAIRY #1

SPECIAL EDITION:
HOLLY THE CHRISTMAS FAIRY

SPECIAL EDITION:
TRIXIE THE HALLOWEEN FAIRY

BEHIND THE MAGIC

DAISY MEADOWS is a pseudonym for the four writers of the internationally best-selling *Rainbow Magic* series: Narinder Dhami, Sue Bentley, Linda Chapman, and Sue Mongredien. *Rainbow Magic* is the no.1 bestselling series for children ages 5 and up with over 40 million copies sold worldwide!

GEORGIE RIPPER was born in London and is a children's book illustrator known for her work on the *Rainbow Magic* series of fairy books. She won the Macmillan Prize for Picture Book Illustration in 2000 with *My Best Friend Bob* and *Little Brown Bushrat*, which she wrote and illustrated.

31901070453792